Dear Dragon Grows a Garden

by Margaret Hillert
Illustrated by David Schimmell

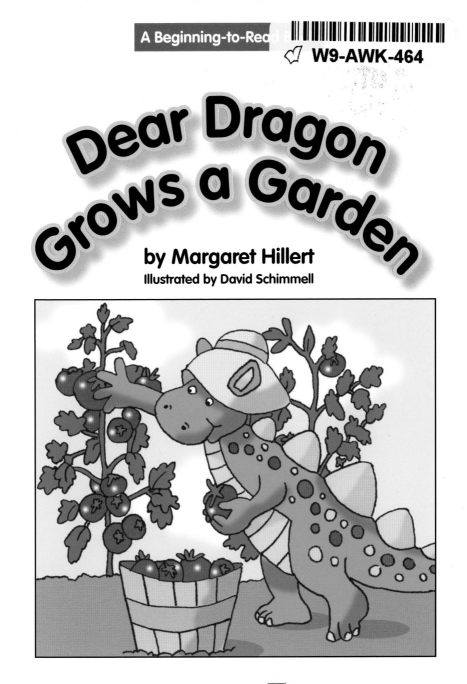

NORWOOD HOUSE PRESS

The **Dear Dragon** series is comprised of carefully written books that extend the collection of classic readers you may remember from your own childhood. Each book features text focused on common sight words. Through the use of controlled text, these books provide young children with abundant practice recognizing the words that appear most frequently in written text. Rapid recognition of high-frequency words is one of the keys for developing automaticity which, in turn, promotes accuracy and rate necessary for fluent reading. The many additional details in the pictures enhance the story and offer opportunities for students to expand oral language and develop comprehension.

Shannon Cannon

Shannon K. Cannon, Ph.D.
Literacy Consultant

Norwood House Press • P.O. Box 316598 • Chicago, Illinois 60631
For more information about Norwood House Press please visit our website at
www.norwoodhousepress.com or call 866-565-2900.

Paperback ISBN: 978-1-60357-414-3

The Library of Congress has cataloged the original hardcover edition with the following call number: 2012043563

This paperback edition was published in 2015.

287R—102015
Printed in ShenZhen, Guangdong, China.

What are you doing, Father?

I am making a spot to grow a garden for good things to eat.
You can help.

Yes, Father.
We can work at this.
We have to dig out the weeds.

Now we do this.

Now we put in some seeds.

We will grow carrots,
tomatoes, and lettuce.
It will make a salad later.

Now we have to wait—
and wait—
and wait.

There will be rain,
then sun.

There will be sun, then rain.

You will sleep and get up.
You will sleep and get up.
You will sleep and get up.

Many days will go by.

And then one day
something little will come up.

Oh, I see it.
I see it.
Something green is in the garden.

And look down here.

Oh, Mother, Mother. Look! We have carrots, tomatoes, and lettuce.

20

That looks good.

Come now.
Sit down and eat.

24

Oh, I like this.
It is so good.

We did good work, Father.
We grew a garden.

Here I am with you.
And here you are with me.
Oh, what good work we did,
Dear Dragon.

WORD LIST

Dear Dragon Grows a Garden **uses the 79 words listed below.**
The **9** words bolded below serve as an introduction to new vocabulary, while the other 70 are pre-primer. You may wish to write the words on index cards and use them to help your child build automatic word recognition. Regular practice with these words will enhance your child's fluency in reading connected text.

a	eat	later	**rain**	up
am		**lettuce**		
and	father	like	**salad**	wait
are	for	little	see	we
at		look(s)	seeds	**weeds**
	garden		sit	what
be	get	make	sleep	will
by	go	making	so	with
	good	many	some	work
can	green	me	something	
carrots	grew	mother	spot	yes
come	**grow**		sun	you
		now		
day(s)	have		that	
dear	help	oh	the	
did	here	one	then	
dig		out	there	
do	I		things	
doing	in	put	this	
down	is		to	
dragon	it		**tomatoes**	

Photograph by Glenna Washburn

ABOUT THE AUTHOR Margaret Hillert has written over 80 books for children who are just learning to read. Her books have been translated into many different languages and over a million children throughout the world have read her books. She first started writing poetry as a child and has continued to write for children and adults throughout her life. A first grade teacher for 34 years, Margaret is now retired from teaching and lives in Michigan where she likes to write, take walks in the morning, and care for her three cats.

ABOUT THE ADVISOR Dr. Shannon Cannon is a teacher educator, in the School of Education at UC Davis where she also earned her Ph.D. in Language, Literacy, and Culture. Currently, she serves on the clinical faculty supervising pre-service teachers and teaching elementary methods courses in reading, effective teaching, and teacher action research. Her own research interests include; early literacy, research-based reading instruction, English learners, culturally responsive teaching, "funds of knowledge" perspectives, neuroscience, social emotional learning, and project-based learning. Shannon began her career in education teaching elementary-aged children in a year-round school. Subsequently, she spent over 15 years in educational publishing developing and writing curricular programs and providing professional development support to classroom teachers across the country.

ABOUT THE ILLUSTRATOR David Schimmell served as a professional firefighter for 23 years before hanging up his boots and helmet to devote himself to working as an illustrator of children's books. David has happily created illustrations for the New Dear Dragon books as well as the artwork for educational and retail book projects. Born and raised in Evansville, Indiana, he lives there today with his wife and family.